For Shaya and Samira Charmatz,
Alan Charmatz, Iona and David,
Priscilla Wong, Tim Heitz, Hannah Go,
Rami Jrade, and Boba and Pica—SC

W

PENGUIN WORKSHOP
An imprint of Penguin Random House LLC, New York

First published in the United States of America by Penguin Workshop, an imprint of Penguin Random House LLC, 2021

Copyright © 2021 by Sean Charmatz

Ocean background photo (pages 32–33): bingokid/E+/Getty Images

Visit us online at penguinrandomhouse.com.

Manufactured in China

ISBN 9780593223796   10 9 8 7 6 5 4 3 2 1

ENDLESS PAWSIBILITIES

by Sean Charmatz

Penguin Workshop

Friendship is never getting annoyed when they want to **paws** for another pic.

It's sharing a **purr**fect **fur**sbee toss.

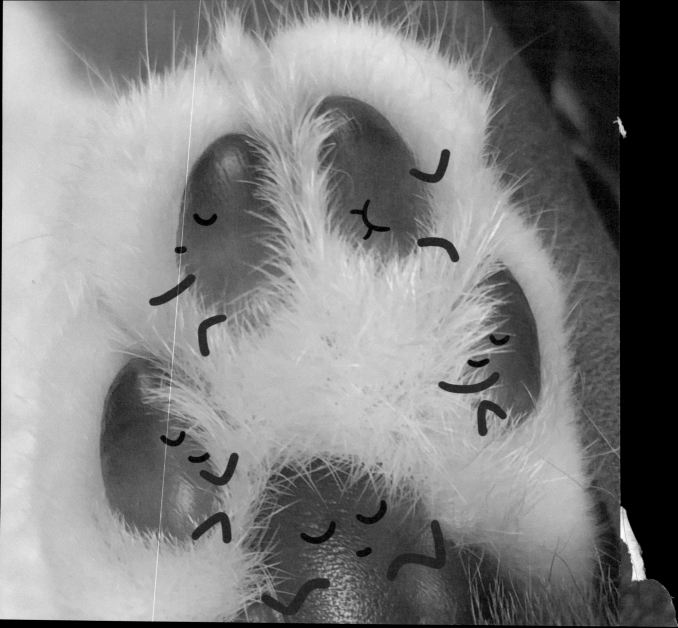

And a litter of **mew**borns keeping each other warm through the night.

Staying cool together on the **fur**st day of summer is **purr**ty sweet.

Friends can spill some juicy **paw**ssip, because they're so trust**fur**thy.

And giving them all the balloons
for **fur**ee is just what you do.

Because friendship is being a**fur**aid of roller coasters, but going on one anyway.

It means offering to be their **purr**sonal trainer.

And **feline** cute together.

Randomly singing together
in perfect har**meow**ny.

Never laughing when they **litter**ally scream at the sight of a spider.

And taking a Ping-Pong match way **mew** seriously!

Friendship is dressing up
and acting like **paw**p stars.

And sharing a surfboard
to **cat**ch a wave.

Playing great **meow**sic
they haaave to hear.

Saving the last bite **fur** them.

And making them **paw**some homemade birthday cards.

Friends always video **cat** with each other, be**claws** a call isn't enough.

And ap**purr**eciate that you **tail** them if there's something in their teeth.

But **meow**stly, friendship is just knowing how **fur**tunate you both are to have each other.

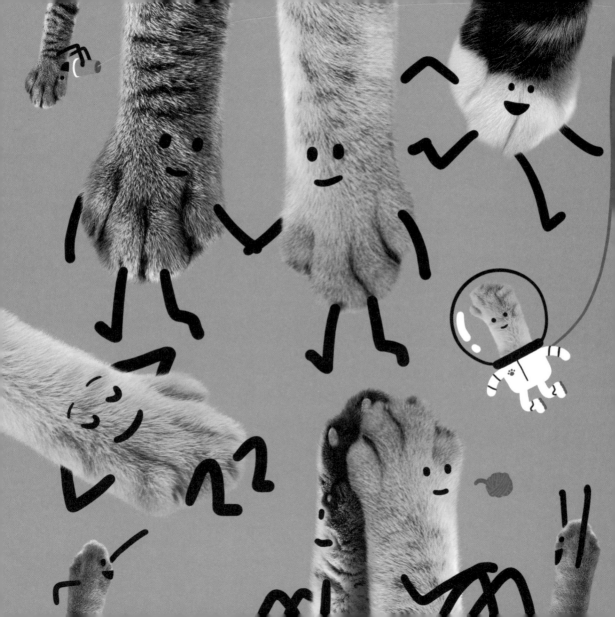